With a hop, a skip, and a hip hip hurrah!
Off to see London with my sweet Baa
We're going to meet the magnificent Queen
In a palace so rich and a park so green

Sad but hopeful, we turned around
Hopped on a bus, going westbound
We drove past bridges and a giant wheel –
A shiny spinning circle made of steel

We zoomed past the Thames, a long and windy river
And buildings so big; cathedrals even bigger
The Tower of London all aglow

As Baa and I waved **Cheerio!**

The Queen stepped out, dressed in blue
With a golden brooch and a lovely hairdo

As the sunset on London's skies
It was time to say our goodbyes
With a hop, a skip and a hip hip hurrah
Oh Baa, how lucky we are

Made in the USA
Las Vegas, NV
28 December 2023

83541945R00017